VINOY THOMAS

TRANSLATED BY NANDAKUMAR K.

ELEPHANTAM MISOPHANTAM

ILLUSTRATED BY SAGAR KOLWANKAR

eka

Published in Malayalam as *Aanatham Piriyatham* in 2021 by D C Books

Published in English as *Elephantam Misophantam* in 2023 by Eka, an imprint of Westland Books, a division of Nasadiya Technologies Private Limited

No. 269/2B, First Floor, 'Irai Arul', Vimalraj Street, Nethaji Nagar, Alapakkam Main Road, Maduravoyal, Chennai 600095

Westland, the Westland logo, Eka and the Eka logo are the trademarks of Nasadiya Technologies Private Limited, or its affiliates.

Copyright © Vinoy Thomas, 2021
Translation copyright © Nandakumar K., 2023

ISBN: 9789357764599

10 9 8 7 6 5 4 3 2 1

This is a work of fiction. Names, characters, organisations, places, events and incidents are either products of the author's imagination or used fictitiously.

All rights reserved

Typeset by Jojy Philip, New Delhi 110 015

Printed at Thomson Press (India) Ltd.

No part of this book may be reproduced, or stored in a retrieval system, or transmitted in any form or by any means, electronic, mechanical, photocopying, recording, or otherwise, without express written permission of the publisher.

ELEPHANTAM MISOPHANTAM

Vinoy Thomas is a native of Iritty, Nellikampoil in north Kerala. A school teacher by profession, he has authored many short story collections, including *Ramachi*, *Mullaranjanam* and *Adiyormishiha enna Novel*. His short story titled 'Ramachi' received the Kerala Sahitya Akademi Award in 2019. His debut novel *Karikottakary* was selected as one of the best novels in a contest held by DC Books. His second novel, *Puttu*, won the Kerala Sahitya Akademi Award in 2021 and has been published in English as *Anthill*.

Vinoy is also a recipient of the Joseph Mundassery Award, VP Shivakumar Memorial Keli Award, Comrade Varghese Memorial Award, Kunhamu Purakkad Memorial Award and the Edakkad Sahitya Vedi Award. He has co-written screenplays for the movies *Paltu Janvar* and *Chaturam*. The movie *Churuli*, made by filmmaker Lijo Jose Pellissery, is based on one of his short stories.

Nandakumar K. is the co-translator of M. Mukundan's *Delhi Gadhakal (Delhi: A Soliloquy)*, which won the JCB Prize for Literature in 2021. His other translations include *A Thousand Cuts*, the autobiography of Prof. T. J. Joseph; *The Lesbian Cow and Other Stories* by Indu Menon; *In the Name of the Lord*, the autobiography of Sr Lucy Kalapura; and *Anthill* (winner of the Kerala Sahitya Akademi Award for the best Malayalam novel in 2021) by Vinoy Thomas.

Contents

1. Tranquiliser Gunslingers — 1
2. The Mischiefs of the Sky and Wind — 8
3. The Whistling Pine Corral — 16
4. Elephantam and Misophantam — 26
5. The Arrival of the Elephant Cloud — 35
6. A Gift for Thithimol — 46
7. The Roving Search Squad — 56
8. The Transformation of the *Mozha* — 64
9. Failcat Tiger — 76
10. Granny Sandalwood Tree — 85
11. Rainbow Tusks — 96

ONE

Tranquiliser Gunslingers

The wild elephant that goes by the name Lightning Tusker must be tranquilised and captured. That was the demand of everyone. The first person Forest Department officials called upon was Dr Printu, an expert user of the tranquiliser dart gun.

In the past, he had brought down many tuskers using darts. But this time, he had to tangle with none less than Lightning Tusker. From the tip of his trunk to the tip of his tail, Lightning Tusker was full of mischief. So the cautious Printu requested his senior and tutor Dr Tharappan to join him.

With new types of darts and a blowgun, he rode in, sprawled inside a swanky car. Swanky cars can't go up the hills where the elephants live. So he had to alight from the car and climb into a jeep, hauling the darts, guns and all.

Seated in the front seat of the jeep, the senior doctor shouted, 'Let the vehicle head for Coconut Hill where Lightning Tusker is standing.'

When we say 'the elephant is standing', don't be under the impression that he was standing there because he was happy doing so. Behind his standing there is a great story of the catch-me-if-you-can game that goes on between the elephants in the wild and the men from the hamlet.

Since there was not enough to eat in the forest, whenever they were hungry, the elephants would come down from the hills and eat whatever they could lay their trunks on. That it was to satisfy their hunger was not a good enough excuse. The hamlet people were losing their crops.

The elephant menace had to be stopped. The Forest Department built an 'elephant wall' along the border of the forest. From the looks of it, it was a super wall. But the workers who built the wall had not mixed enough cement in the concrete. So how did it fare? When the elephants' bodies grazed against the wall, it began to crumble and collapse in many places.

The previous afternoon, when Lightning Tusker had passed by the wall, he had noticed a huge gap in it. It was easy for him to step in through the breach and enter the coconut grove belonging to Churuttyalan Shreedharan. Without giving it a second thought, he ambled into the grove. His plan was to dig up and topple the palms and eat the tender leaflets.

It was in broad daylight. And the people were watching. Won't they scream and run hither and thither announcing the elephant is in the grove? They did run helter-skelter and shrieked. And that's how the Forest Department officials, who were on the lookout for an opportunity to catch Lightning Tusker, called for Dr Printu.

While they were waiting for him and his tutor to reach, Lightning Tusker had to be stopped from returning to the forest. The public is good only for shouting and bickering; they aren't capable of stopping elephants like Lightning. That was left to the forest wardens and trainer elephants or *kumkis*. By late evening, they were after him in right earnest.

The forest wardens stacked big trees in all the breaks in the wall and set them on fire. Five or six kumkis were made to stand at various points in the coconut grove.

If Lightning made a move in any direction, the kumkis headed him off and blocked his way. Thus, with the ring of fire and ring of elephants, they kept Lightning at bay for the whole night.

Now that the shooters had come with their tranquilizer guns, everyone expected the tusker to be corralled within a short time.

As soon as the tutor stepped down from the jeep to take a look at the tusker, a drop of water fell on the nape of his neck.

Wondering where the water was coming from, Dr Tharappan looked up at the heavens. The sight that met their eyes sent a shiver through both the tutor and his student.

The entire sky was full of dark, puffy rain clouds seemingly bursting with water.

'Hey Printu, when we got into the jeep, we had bright sunshine. Where did so many clouds gather from in the blink of an eye?'

'Who knows! It's fickle weather,' the clueless Dr Printu blamed the weather gods.

This was a different kettle of fish. They were supposed to catch Lightning, no less. Could the heavens stay uninvolved? No way! The heavens opened up, starting their own game. The rain came down with such din and uproar that it drowned even the bellowing of elephants.

Dr Tharappan thought that the meddlesome, senseless rain choosing that hour to do its stuff could lead to many problems. He expressed his thoughts immediately in so many words.

'Printu, it's a wall of water! Where are we supposed to shoot, and at what?'

'Sir, we need to be careful. If the elephant is coming this way, we won't even be able to see it.' Though Printu's words were not heard by Dr Tharappan, Lightning heard them. Deciding that was what he should do, the tusker started to walk towards the veterinarians.

The tutor, being a tutor after all, picked up the loaded tranquiliser gun. He grabbed it planning to take a shot as soon as the rain eased, although before shooting he had to first locate the elephant.

He asked his student to follow and stepped forward. He wiped his forehead to clear the water that was cascading over his eyes. He placed his hand on his eyebrows to block the waterfall and squinted.

Lightning Tusker was missing from the spot he was last seen.

'*Uyy-baapre*, terrible guy, where has he disappeared?' He asked, not expecting his student to hear him.

But his disciple did hear him.

'Sir, people say he has magical powers, can cloak and fade. I am starting to feel afraid.'

Blinding rain continued to fall around them. The tutor too got nervous now. The brave tutor moved close to the student; the intrepid student sidled closer to him.

'Printu, don't be afraid. Haven't I handled so many elephants?' The tutor tried to reassure his disciple.

'Have you dealt with elephants in such rains?'

The tutor turned to the side in preparation to tell a gross lie in reply. But the sight that met him in the next instant turned him speechless with fright.

The jeep they had travelled in was aloft about four or five feet in the air. In between its wheels were two tusks that flashed like lightning.

The sight made Dr Printu scream in fear. He ran and leapt down from the top of the rock. At the end of that rash leap, he hit the ground beneath the rock. But before

he could count the injuries wrought upon his body, he saw the smashed and torn-up jeep flying over his head and into the valley.

After he had flung the jeep down, Lightning could not decide what to do next. He too was in a daze.

He stood on top of the cliff and gazed down for some time. Other than the wrecked jeep, nothing else could be seen. Then he turned around and started to run.

Dr Printu believed that the tusker was running because he had seen his tutor and that his mentor may not survive to take another shot at the elephant.

But the elephant had sped off due to another reason. Since it was raining bucketloads, the fires lit by the forest wardens had died down. Lightning was planning to use this opportunity to flee into the forest through the gap in the wall.

All the kumkis who stood with their muscles bunched up to stop Lightning were unnerved by his minatory ear-splitting trumpeting and the speed at which he ran. Lightning was looking straight ahead at the forest on a dead run.

He was relieved when he reached the breach in the wall. All the fires there had died down. He lifted and flung away the burnt trees lying there. Loudly trumpeting once more in joy, he stepped into the gap.

Little did he know that a danger greater than fire awaited him.

TWO

The Mischiefs of the Sky and Wind

When he leapt towards the forest with a booming bellow, in his excitement, Lightning's eyes closed momentarily. Even if his eyes were open, it would not have made a difference—the rain was still coming down heavily, growling and snarling. He could not have seen what lay ahead.

If he had seen it, he would not have dashed forth. And the spikes would not have pierced his trunk and the top of his head. And his tusks would not have been impaled by the rail fence.

The rail fence was a recent invention. Rails were cut into pieces about twelve feet high, placed vertically close to each other and driven into the ground. Then, iron spikes were welded on to the rails. Elephants who tried to drive their tusks into them got stuck like Lightning now was.

The previous night, the wily forest wardens had erected the rail fence behind the fires they had lit up. A treacherous double fence. Even if Lightning managed to run through the fire, he would not be able to escape into the forest. That was the purpose.

Lightning watched as the blood from his wounds inflicted by the barbs mixed with rainwater and flowed down. If only he could pull his tusks out of the spikes, his head would also be freed. Lightning tried hard to pull himself free.

Although in one way the rains had come as a blessing for Lightning Tusker, his feet were slipping over the slush on the forest floor, and so he couldn't find enough grip to free himself. After straining for some time, he felt tired.

There was a reason for it. Dr Tharappan had started to flee when he saw Lightning with the jeep held over his head. But the timely realisation that he was carrying a dart gun loaded with a powerful tranquilizer gave him some courage.

As courage seeped into him slowly and he turned around and looked, he saw Lightning racing away with the jeep still aloft. He thought Lightning was trying to fling the jeep at the fleeing Dr Printu.

Shouting 'You foul elephant, are you attacking Printu?', Dr Tharappan lifted his gun, and, without

taking aim, shot at the elephant. He was sure he wasn't going to miss the mark.

And sure enough, he didn't miss it—the dart pierced the muscles of Lightning's front leg.

While Dr Tharappan was trying to hide behind a tree, the bark of which resembled crocodile skin, he smiled—a smile of relief.

The drug that had entered the tusker's leg would now dash around like a caged rat and run up all the way into the elephant's brain and give it one heavy huff. With that, the elephant would lose consciousness.

Lightning started to feel tired when the drug kicked in. But he wasn't an ordinary elephant who'd faint just like that. Would he not receive help from some quarters?

He lifted his head and looked up at the sky, blinking. The sky saw the look he gave it. *Poor tusker, I must help him.*

Lo and behold, suddenly like glucose-infused water, a coloured medicinal rain started to fall in spurts from the heavens, only at the spot where Lightning Tusker stood!

The rain fell on Lightning's head at first. As if instructed on the path to take, it directly flowed into the wounds made by the barbs.

With his eyes shut, Lightning was quietly receiving the rain into his body. If Dr Tharappan's drug had dashed like a caged rat through the elephant's veins, this antidote sprinted like a cat chasing the rat.

The tranquiliser was waiting hesitantly and wondering if it should get into the elephant's brain. Calming drugs are always sluggish anyway; they take their own sweet time. This sight gladdened the heart of the magic medicine coming up behind. Now the sluggard can do nothing!

All the actions thereafter were performed by the magic medicine. It caught Dr Tharappan's drug in its jaws. It shook and swung it till its bones rattled and it collapsed like a heap of slayed jelly. Then it was pushed down through the tusker's veins.

Pushing and shoving, the magic medicine brought the corpse of the tranquiliser till the elephant's pee-pee. And from there, with one kick, it was sent tumbling down.

The moment Cheramban Mooppan saw the coloured rain falling only on Lightning, he exclaimed, 'The heavens have started their performance!'

When he saw Lightning pass a potful of urine, he was sure.

'Now he'll be back to his old self. They won't be able to shackle him.'

When Dr Tharappan heard that, he said, 'Is that so? Then I will shoot him with this. Let him die!' Before anyone could blink, he filled the dart with enough drug to knock out three elephants and loaded it into the gun.

With his strength regained, thanks to the healing rain from the sky, in one tug, Lightning freed his trunk and tusks from the spikes and his head from the barbed fence.

Trumpeting menacingly, he swivelled towards the kumkis who were trying to approach him.

Dr Tharappan needed only that instant. He lifted the gun nonchalantly and shot at Lightning. The dart found its mark again.

This time too, when the drug was about to reach his brain, Lightning looked up at the heavens. But the sky didn't have anything to neutralise so much drug. Taking pity on the tusker, it expressed its sympathy and bawled through a flash of lightning.

Realising that the sky was helpless, Lightning bowed his head and looked at the kumkis. They rushed to him and supported him from all sides so that he wouldn't fall down.

They knew what was to be done next. They eagerly led him towards the tree with the crocodile-skin bark. Lightning's head stayed bowed.

The forest wardens and the brave mahouts tiptoed, slinked and approached Lightning warily. Even if drugged, it was still Lightning Tusker—how could they not be afraid?

They had already kept ready a fetter twice as thick as the regular chains used to tie elephants. As soon as they saw that Lightning Tusker had been tranquilised, they fetched the fetter.

Standing away from the tree and flinging hawsers tied to the fetter and pulling it, they finally managed to get the chain around Lightning Tusker's leg. The fetter was fastened to the crocodile-bark tree. The wardens as well as the public let out a sigh of relief. At last, Lightning Tusker had been tethered.

Everyone looked gratefully towards Dr Tharappan. The doctor bowed his head acknowledging the thanksgiving.

Someone asked, 'Wasn't there one more doctor here?'

Everyone thought of Printu only then. They went in all directions in search of him.

Dr Tharappan was indignant that instead of honouring him adequately, everyone had gone looking for Printu. Considering this was in the nature of all seniors, the people did not heed it at all.

Shackled to the tree, Lightning Tusker didn't have the strength to look up at the sky. But the sky was witness to everything. It rained down torrents of water, spitting angrily on those who fancied that they could tether and corral Lightning for a lark.

Watching the mood and manner of the rain, Cheramban Mooppan, seated beneath the Palmyra palm, said, 'This is some rain! Watch out, many more things are on the way.'

THREE

The Whistling Pine Corral

The efforts to catch Lightning Tusker were not a recent development. For the past two or three years, whenever he came to their settlement and wreaked havoc, the villagers would say, '*Arrrgh*, the damned elephant pulled out this; he stomped on that; he wrecked this; he razed that; he knocked this down; he tried to impale me on his tusks …'

It was one complaint after another. Eventually, the government's decision came six months ago. The order said that Lightning Tusker be tranquilised, chained with the help of kumkis, corralled, disciplined and turned into a tame elephant.

The preparations began in earnest. Brobdingnagian trainer jumbos were brought in from different places. The sharpshooters among the tranquiliser gunners were summoned.

Cutting down sturdy whistling pine trees that had no bore holes, a corral as tall as an elephant was built. A twelve-wheel truck stood ready with a wooden stockade on its platform to carry away the elephant.

A special squad of forest wardens led by a hook-moustachioed ranger was formed.

After all these preparations had been made, when they started to get bored from having to sit idle, twiddling their thumbs, Lightning Tusker descended again from the forest, impelled by a craving for tender coconut leaflets. Crowds gathered, there was hullabaloo, and matters reached this stage.

Lightning, now chained to the crocodile-skin bark tree, had to be taken to the stockade in the forest office around twelve kilometres away. Hook Moustache called for the twelve-wheel truck to be brought around.

Chortling, the giant truck started moving towards Coconut Hill to load the elephant. Lightning was still standing with his head bowed. He hadn't lost his consciousness fully. Let alone move around, he wasn't even able to lift his head. Meanwhile, the sky continued to wail, accompanied by lightning and thunder.

To see if he had enough strength to lift his head, Lightning moved his trunk a bit. The air surrounding the trunk swirled around. A tear from Lightning's eye fell into that vortex of air.

When the tear hit it, the heart of the wind writhed in agony. Wind and Lightning Tusker were bosom friends.

While he was in the forest, it was Wind who rushed in every time and warned him of the smell of approaching humans.

On Lightning's magnificent tusks were inscribed stories about the smells of lands where there was no air. Lightning would narrate those stories to Wind. When you have been constant companions like that, can one bear to see the other in danger?

Lightning's captivity was unbearable to Wind. Also to many creatures in the forest and the village. The small vortex into which Lightning's tear drop had fallen turned into a whirlwind.

'Go on, Wind, go and spiral like there is no tomorrow,' an earthworm said, just before it eased itself into the ground.

'Do something, Wind. The twelve-wheeler is coming,' the babbler bird flew in and exhorted.

The crocodile-skin bark tree joined in the chorus excitedly, 'Even if it means my getting uprooted, you try and save Lightning.'

These words were enough to energise the wind. It gained power and started to whirl faster. Whirling in that fashion, it turned into a thundering typhoon, the likes of which that land had never seen.

Its first act was to shake the crocodile-skin bark tree to its roots and dislodge it. The shackle on Lightning's leg, which had been fastened to the tree, fell loose.

Afraid that the tree may fall on them, the terrified kumkis shrieked piteously, 'Save us, help us!' Their shrieks enraged the wind. It shook itself like a wet dog getting rid of water after a bath and rose up high.

What followed was a dance of destruction. Huge trees were felled all across the road on which the twelve-wheeler was travelling. Electric posts were tossed up like matchsticks and flung away, the cables trailing behind. A wild oak tree flew up and crashed on the forest wardens' nasty jeep.

Watching all this, Chembaran Mooppan said, 'Guys, let him go. Don't try to catch him.'

But Hook Moustache only laughed. There's only so much the wind can do. After it's done huffing and puffing, we will do as planned.

Hook Moustache had charted out what was to be done once the wind had played itself out.

The first thing done was to call everyone who owned mechanised wood-saws. Now, which woodcutter would not heed the summons of a forest officer? Everyone turned up—about twenty-five of them—bearing electric and chain saws that go *krrrr ... krrrrr ...* Within no time, all the trees that had fallen on the road were cut into logs and removed, clearing the way for the twelve-wheeler.

When the wind went down, the kumkis regained their courage. Propping up Lightning, who was now unchained after the crocodile-bark tree had fallen, they started their fun and games once more. That sight reminded Hook Moustache of the need to chain Lightning again.

Hook Moustache knew every tree that grew in the forest. About four hundred metres away from the crocodile-skin bark tree was an old, very old, crotchety, stunted jackfruit tree.

At the top of the tree was a mushroom flower in full bloom. Mushroom flowers can be found only on trees with roots that run deep into the netherworld and suck the blue water there.

This time, Hook Moustache had chosen a tree that would not get uprooted no matter how strong the wind.

The kumkis nudged and prodded and pushed Lightning till the wild jackfruit tree. The wardens got busy throwing the hawsers and soon managed to chain Lightning to the tree.

As Lightning stood leaning against it, the hoary wild jackfruit tree whispered a question through its heartbeat into his head. Lightning didn't understand what was said.

It was late evening. Lightning had to be taken to the corral before nightfall. Hook Moustache kept calling and egging the twelve-wheeler to reach them quickly.

'The tree trunks have been moved, but all the branches and boughs and twigs and sprigs are all lying around. I can't speed up the vehicle,' the driver told the ranger.

'Oh, okay, get here fast, whichever way you can! We have to finish this thing before it gets dark,' Hook Moustache goaded the driver.

Skipping over and brushing and scraping against the branches and twigs, the twelve-wheeler somehow reached the spot. Now the kumkis had to push and shove Lightning into the truck. Two wardens leapt down from it to unchain Lightning. When they were about to unhook the chain, they looked at each other in astonishment.

'Man, it's only half-an-hour or forty-five minutes at the most that he has been chained to this tree. How did it become like this?'

'Is it that this chain was already here?' the second warden asked.

The tree trunk had grown around the chain as if it had been tied to it for over a hundred years. In fact, the chain seemed to be growing out of the tree.

'Sir, what should we do?' the warden asked.

Cheramban Mooppan warned again. 'Leave him be, he is no ordinary elephant.'

Hook Moustache laughed aloud. 'Quite simple. If you can't find the hook, cut the chain.'

He phoned welders and ironsmiths. He called repeatedly. When they turned up, there were at least five each in each category. They cut the chain within the time given to them. But none of them noticed a red resin leaking from the foot of the wild jackfruit tree.

When Lightning started to stir a little, everyone grew nervous. If he regained consciousness everything would turn topsy-turvy. Everything was speeded up, therefore.

The kumkis shoulder-charged and pushed Lightning into the twelve-wheeler, and the journey began with a tired Lightning leaning against the stockade on the truck. It took thirty minutes to reach the forest office. The kumkis reached there too, and, prodding Lightning with their tusks, made him climb down from the truck.

The rain had stopped. As planned by Hook Moustache, they succeeded in getting Lightning into the corral before sundown. However, they could not rest easy. Night would fall soon, and Lightning was no ordinary elephant.

The members of the special squad posted themselves around the corral. To keep their fear at bay, fires had to be lit. Everything had been arranged for, including the kindling.

Only when night fell did Hook Moustache realise that it was a full moon night. That was a relief. The forest bathed in moonlight would lessen the dread of the wardens.

However, even in the brightest moonlight, there was one creature that could move through the forest unseen by anyone: Granny Elephant, the queen of all elephants.

Old as the hills, the hoary Granny was a wanderlust. She never remained in any forest for long and moved around all the time. She was returning from one of her long tours tonight. As soon as she entered this forest, the baby elephants gathered around her to listen to her tales. The news of Lightning Tusker being corralled was given to her by these baby elephants.

When she heard it, she laughed gently and continued to walk. The baby elephants could not make out why she had laughed. She was already striding ahead. The baby elephants trotted behind her on their short legs. She told them that while travelling in the night, they should not make any noise, not even as soft as a leaf falling. They obeyed her.

Though the party was meandering and had no set destination, when the moonlight was at its brightest, they ended up near the corral where Lightning was being held.

A little away from the forest office, where the light from the small bonfires could not reach, Granny stood and gazed at the corral.

Inside it, Lightning was slowly returning to his senses. The air carried the vintage smell of Granny to him. He grunted softly.

Hearing his call, Granny lifted her trunk and sent out a caress into the air. Lightning caught that caress. Granny released a bunch of soundless words into the air after that. Wind delivered them to Lightning without missing a pause or a sigh or a comma or a period.

'Granny, what did you tell Lightning mama?' the baby elephants asked her.

'Only told him—son, don't be sad.'

With the serene grace of a moonrise, Granny lifted her leg and stepped forward.

'But, Gran, who won't feel sad when captured and bundled into a cage like this? Even if you are the elephant queen, must you say such meaningless words?' demanded one of the baby elephants known for his impertinent backanswering.

Granny shook with silent laughter. The baby elephants did not realise that it was laughter. Not too worried about that, she said, 'You little dumbos, have you noticed his tusks? Do you think an ordinary elephant can have such tusks? No one can cage him and tame him. He will escape with the ease of plucking out grass. Do you all understand?'

She continued to laugh. Now the baby elephants realised that she was laughing.

'Are you sure, Gran?' the youngest she-elephant among them asked.

'Umm, yes.' Granny continued to laugh.

'How are you so sure?' Another she-elephant baby wound her trunk around Granny's leg.

'Because he has Elephantam in him. He cannot be subdued.'

'Elephantam? What's that?' All of them wanted to know.

Granny paused at the top of the hill that they were going to climb down and looked back at them. Widening their tiny eyes, the baby elephants looked at her, anxious to learn what Elephantam was.

FOUR

Elephantam and Misophantam

Lightning could sense that Granny and the baby elephants were still in the forest. He was glad that they had visited him. But what if the wardens heard them and did something to hurt them! So he sent them a silent message, 'All of you go away quickly, run!'

Granny understood his concern. She gathered the baby elephants and started to walk back.

'Gran, the whole forest knows you are a big talker. Isn't that why you keep saying that he has Elephantam, that Lightning mama will escape and such things?' said one of the elephant babies, famous for his reverence towards elders.

Another one, as reverential as the first one, said, 'Gran, instead of fooling us, tell us if you found some place where there are delicious things to eat.'

Granny stood there laughing. She had seen so many places that had good things to eat and drink. The mouth-watering, sweet smell when the red bark of the lime tree was pulled out ... the succulent jackfruit that came out when a *varikka chakka* was tossed up and caught, mashed gently and dropped into the mouth ... the thrill when a plantain tree was crushed underfoot along with the bunches of ripe bananas and gathered up in the trunk and chewed on, releasing the tangy sap ... the honey-like taste of the red bunches of *muttipazham*, that festooned the tree from top to bottom, after they were nuzzled with the trunk, plucked and tossed into the mouth ...

On moonlit nights, in the blue pond deep inside the forest, slightly sour water could be found. If a few trunkfuls of the water were guzzled down, for two days she would get such a high that she might as well be floating in the air ...

Although many such things came to her mind, Granny did not tell any of it to the baby elephants.

'You chumps, what is important is not eating and drinking.'

'Then what the hell is the real thing?' A she-baby elephant known for her politeness posed the question.

Granny was only too keen that she be asked questions by the little ones. The impertinence of the questions or the irreverence in their phrasing did not matter. She walked along the side of the hill for a little while. The baby elephants brought up the rear.

'Is everything that matters found in Elephantam? Honestly?'

'If that is so, Gran, tell us what Elephantam is.'

Impatient, the baby elephants overtook her and stood facing her. Granny stopped walking and gazed at the stillness of the moonlight that blanketed the hill.

'The history of Elephantam starts a long, long time ago.'

'How long ago?' One of the baby elephants asked.

'The beginning of time. The beginning of the universe. It's the story of two powers wrestling with each other. Do you want to hear it?'

'Yes, yes, we want to hear!' When the baby elephants started to clamour thus, Granny began to narrate the stories that had been passed down the generations among the elephant clan.

'It was long ago, when there was no history. There was nothing at the time, only dust. That dust somehow turned into a vortex. A vortex spins. This one spun like a top. Spinning like that, all the dust coalesced into a massive universe.

'Although all the dust cohered and turned into the universe, it didn't stop spinning. *Trrrr … Trrrr …* it continued to spin. While it kept spinning like that, a noble thing and a wicked thing happened.

'The noble thing was that all the goodness and love that lay scattered in different corners of the universe found one another and turned into an embodiment of all that is good. It took the form of a black elephant. That was Elephantam—the essence of everything that was good and noble in the world.

'However, this universe comprises not only goodness and love; it has wickedness and hatred too. As the universe continued to spin, evil powers too coalesced together. They too took the shape of an elephant. A blindingly white elephant. That was Misophantam.

'Wickedness is driven by the wish to divide everyone and create ill will. That got the white elephant this name.

'Misophantam wanted to destroy Elephantam and take over the universe. So it kept fighting with Elephantam.

'That was the mother of all wars. A war that endured through the ages.

'At first, Misophantam released poisonous air. Hotter than fire, it turned the universe red hot. Everything started to melt.

'Can the universe be surrendered to hatred and wickedness? Elephantam decided to counter Misophantam. He blew winds colder than snow, an antidote to the poisonous air. The universe started to cool down.

'Aha, let me show you what I can do, said Misophantam and started its next gambit. Cackling loudly, it wantonly released rays of wickedness. The electric rays singed the universe and burned it up.

'Elephantam had its own counter. It spread a blanket of darkness over the universe. Unable to find their way through the darkness, the wicked rays bounced off the mantle and Misophantam lost that battle too.

'All these attacks and defences happened over many eons. When Misophantam found that none of its ploys were working, it was furious beyond measure. Enraged, Misophantam started to stomp through the innards of the universe. Its heavy steps were strong enough to shatter the universe. The shockwaves made the universe tremble. It started to roll around as if it had lost all moorings. Elephantam decided it could not let things go on in this fashion. There had to be a resolution, one way or the other. Misophantam had to be stopped from trampling on everything. That was a terrible war. One that stretched over many eons.

'In the end, Elephantam succeeded in stopping the galumphing of Misophantam. Using its trunks and legs, Elephantam trussed up Misophantam and rendered it immobile. No one was able to calculate how long it was kept like that.

'Being in limbo enabled Misophantam to become more powerful. Elephantam tightened its stranglehold so that Misophantam would not break loose. And at the end of this tussle between an immovable object and an irresistible force, it happened ...

'Bi ... biii ... big ... the Big Bang!

'An explosion. No explosion that powerful had happened before. Nor will it happen again. In that fierce explosion, the universe broke up into countless pieces. That was how the sun, earth, stars, moon, planets and other heavenly bodies came into being. The fight between Elephantam and Misophantam still continues. Sometimes Misophantam wins; other times Elephantam does.

'Elephantam is all about goodness and love. It has to keep doing good things.

'Elephantam climbs into the skies and lights up the stars. Misophantam can't bear that sight. It will go up and snuff out the stars.

'Elephantam will paint beautiful pictures in the sky. Misophantam will dash around and scratch and rub them out.

'Elephantam will blow air into the moon, make it large. Misophantam will gnaw at the moon and ruin its roundness.

'Misophantam would be dashing around everywhere. So when this earth was formed, it came rushing and settled down here. Which is why all life on earth got separated into trees, plants, insects, animals, birds, humans and became divergent.

'But Misophantam alone is not enough on this earth. Therefore, Elephantam too puts in an appearance every now and then. It rides on clouds that are shaped like

elephants. When it sees the state of things on this earth, it weeps. A teardrop or two will fall to the earth then. A drop of its tears is enough for Elephantam to survive in this world, openly and covertly, for centuries.'

Lost in her thoughts, Granny continued to walk in silence for some time. She ended up at the top of the tallest hill in the area. From there, she could see the forest below bathed in moonlight and the sky above with its clouds, moon and stars.

'These teardrops that fall occasionally on our earth give elephants their "elephanthood", humans their "humanity", tigers their "tigerliness" and vines their "vineliness". Elephantam never ceases to be. If you watch closely, you will find it in everything.'

'True, isn't this forest like a big herd of elephants?' a baby elephant asked.

'The sky too has Elephantam,' said one who was gazing at the clouds.

'Look at the rocks over there—absolutely Elephantam.'

'The shining moon bears it too.'

Granny was happy to hear how sensible the elephant babies sounded. Caressing the ones standing close to her, she said, 'We are the lucky ones; we can see Elephantam in its real form. If we look at his tusks, we can see Elephantam.'

'Whose tusks?' interjected a baby elephant who had not been paying attention till then.

'Lightning Tusker's. He wasn't born just like that.' Granny's voice was brimming with pride as she said that.

The baby elephant that stood nuzzling against Granny asked, 'How was Lightning mama born?'

'I'll tell you.' Granny Elephant recalled how Elephantam reached the earth.

FIVE

The Arrival of the Elephant Cloud

Five or six forest wardens were seated in front of the corral, basking in the heat from the fire. Looking at them seated with their teeth clenched, cheeks puffed out and eyes bulging, everyone would have thought they were alert and intently guarding Lightning Tusker. On the contrary, most of them were asleep. But none of them were snoring.

Suddenly, one of the wardens was startled out of his sleep. An astonishing sight greeted him when he looked towards the corral.

Two curved bridges seemed to be rising from the top of the corral and touching the moon. They were shining. As the warden kept gazing at it, it appeared to him that they were not bridges but two rivers. Two rivers of light.

He shook awake the warden posted next to him.

'Da, is that a bridge or a river?'

'What?' the other warden asked as if he was never asleep.

'Can't you see the thing climbing up from the corral?'

'Man, aren't they the elephant's tusks? They are not climbing up. They are just there. Are you drunk or something?'

'It's not that. Please watch it closely. Doesn't it look like it's moving up?'

The other warden peered closely. There was nothing like what his neighbour had said; nothing was becoming longer. However, he too felt that those tusks looked menacing.

They went back to sleep comforting themselves with the thought that after all it was night-time, they were in a forest, such delusions could happen.

But atop the hill, Granny and the baby elephants were staring at the tusks that looked as if they were flowing down from the moon.

'Little ones, look at those tusks. Everything is inscribed on them,' Granny said, gently slapping two baby elephants who were distracted. After that, they too looked up at the light flowing from the tusks.

As the baby elephants stood gazing at the tusks, they appeared to grow bigger and bigger. There were stories written all over them.

The baby elephants wanted to hear Lightning Tusker's story. As they stood flapping their ears patiently, without

Granny narrating it, they started to hear Lightning Tusker's story.

It was a few elephant years ago. That means, before Lightning Tusker's own father was born. As per the elephant calendar, it was a blazing hot month. As per the Malayalam calendar, it was the zenith of summer.

Sheets of flame were descending from the sky. Fear spread in both the forests and in human settlements that they would run out of water—there wouldn't be enough to have a decent bath and maybe even to drink.

Even if there was no water, would people stop parading elephants for temple festivals? No. Everywhere the elephants were goaded and whipped and made to stand and walk in the scorching heat as humans celebrated.

Even if the senseless humans were doing insensitive things, Elephantam would not allow the forests and the hamlets to go up in smoke, would it?

Whenever it looked as if everything was going to perish in the heat, from the south-western corner of the earth, an elephant-shaped breeze would start to blow. It would turn into a strong wind and arrive, flying at a regal speed, like a freighter filled with billowing rain clouds, cold, lightning, thunder, and so on.

Elephantam would be hidden somewhere deep inside this mammoth wind.

That year, when the elephantine wind arrived at the height of dogdays, everyone was happy and relieved. Rains would cool everything down.

However, the Elephantam present inside the clouds was very sad. As it looked down, everything it saw caused it only heartache.

The elephants in the forests had nothing to eat or drink. Starvation had reduced them to mere skin and bones, and they were wandering around aimlessly. The wild elephants had to suffer starvation, all right, but what about the tamed elephants under human care? In the blazing heat of a fiery summer, the soles of their feet blistered and cracked because they had to walk on baking-hot concrete and on roads with melted tar. On their legs were festering wounds caused by the shackles and spiked chains that they were forced to wear. Mahouts would poke the wounds occasionally with their sharp *ankusha* or goad sticks.

Their ears were all torn from the hook of the ankusha and the elephants could not even flap them to cool themselves. When they stood in front of huge multi-prong flambeaus, the heat and smoke blinded them. To make things worse, they had to suffer the clamour of the humans, the ear-splitting beating of chendas and the bursting of crackers and other heavy fireworks.

Although it had been witnessing such sights every year, somehow that year Elephantam could not hold back the tears.

Flying over other lands, it may have wept in the past, but this was the first time Elephantam's tear was being spilt on this land. We may call it a 'tear', but it is not a liquid. Consider it a slice of ur-love.

Though Elephantam had begun to feel weepy when the rain clouds and winds had moved in overland from the sea, the tear fell to the earth much after that.

We cannot term it as 'falling'. This was something in existence since the time the universe was formed. It may have been floating or flying or anything like that.

It first hit the dome of a temple. As soon as it hit, it bounced off the dome into the air. Next it hit the searchlight on the big top of a circus tent; then the water tank of a house; from there, the crucifix of a church. Bouncing and skipping in this fashion, it travelled till the sky above the forest.

That was when it heard someone crying. When it went down to take a look, it saw that it was the sound of water caught inside a small rocky pool. If measured, the water would add up to a litre. It was bawling.

Since Elephantam knew the language of water, it asked, 'Why are you bawling like this?'

Though the litre of water heard the question, she could not see the questioner. However, etiquette required her to give a reply.

'I am caught in this rocky hollow. Do you have any idea how far I need to travel?'

Earlier, when that litre of water had left the sea and joined the rain clouds, her mother had told her, 'Baby, go and see the world and come back. Your amma will be waiting for you here.' Once upon a time, the mother too had joined the wind, travelled, flowed down the hill, joined a stream, then a river, and reached the sea. The mother had told her daughter how to return home.

Sitting by the side of the hollow, Elephantam asked the litre of water, 'Where do you have to reach?'

'From here I have to reach the stream. From there I must flow into the river. Thereafter, the river will carry me. I have to reach my mother.' The litre of water started to wail, though she could still not see who she was speaking to.

Elephantam, after all, is our ur-love. Lamentation of this sort is something that Elephantam cannot bear. Without giving it further thought, he went into the hollow and joined the litre of water. The moment Elephantam joined it, the litre of water rose up, leapt out of the rocky hollow and started to flow.

However, from that instant on, she forgot her desire to re-join the sea and meet her mother. Elephantam had joined her; nothing else was needed any more.

As we know, the elephants of that forest were already on a summer starvation diet. When they saw the rains arrive, the skin-and-bones herd climbed down to the parched meadow and started to frolic in the showers.

A cow-elephant, into the second month of her pregnancy, was among them. Though emaciated, and forgetting the fatigue of pregnancy, she started to dance in the rain. After some time, she felt thirsty.

As it fell, the rain was drumming out a tune ... *I am here ... I am here ...* but the elephants could not get enough water into their trunks. The elephants who were getting drenched looked around—they saw nothing other than rain water. That was when they heard the sounds of flowing water coming from below the hill.

Trumpeting and snorting in glee, they ran down the hill. The pregnant cow-elephant was leading the charge.

By the time they reached the river, it was in full flow. The hole from which they usually drank water was full too.

Though she had started off in the front, by the time they arrived at the river, the pregnant elephant was behind everyone. But when she reached the riverbank, all the other elephants made way for her. She stepped down into the hole, filled her trunk and sprayed the water into the air.

She twirled her trunk once more inside the water and took in enough to quench her thirst. The water she was about to drink now would be the tastiest. She drank greedily.

How delicious! She thought the great taste was the product of her thirst. But that wasn't the reason. The water she drank had Elephantam mixed in it.

When that litre of water went inside the cow-elephant, the teeny-weeny tusker that was taking shape in her womb felt astonishment, fear, happiness or something like that. A magical water was enveloping him. He felt a tickle and a thrill run through him as he lay with his eyes closed.

In that tickly state, he wasn't aware of the passage of the rainy season, winter, spring and summer. He was also not aware that the magical water that was swirling around him had entered him and turned him into a magical elephant.

By the time he was ready to pop from his mother's womb, his tiny head, tiny legs, tiny tummy, tiny trunk, tiny everything was full of Elephantam. The little tusker was born when the trees and plants were in full bloom and the forest was a riot of indescribable colours.

To deliver him, accompanied by another cow-elephant, his mother went to a meadow which had no tree stumps or rocks or boulders. It was approaching evening and a flock of birds reached the meadow.

They flew over the meadow, criss-crossing it and singing:

> *Elephantam … Elephantam …*
> *That's where you and I are one …*
> *The happy forest and land sing in unison ...*
> *Elephantam … Elephantam …*

Laughing happily, the mother elephant stretched out her trunk towards the birds and waved at them.

After that, richly-coloured butterflies arrived. They flitted around in the meadow. That evening, the flowers that normally closed after sunset bloomed wider when the sun went down.

After the sun disappeared behind the hills and the sky was awash in crimson and scarlet, the baby tusker started to slide out of his mother's womb.

All the elephants were in attendance, waiting at the top and bottom of the meadow. They stood there as if awaiting a miracle.

It was indeed a miracle. The little tusker was born with extraordinary characteristics unseen in elephants from time immemorial. A celestial light of a billion hues spread in the sky.

As she stood below a stunted tree at the top of the meadow and watched all this happening, tears started to roll down from the eyes of the Granny Elephant of that era. She was thinking of all the troubles the baby tusker would have to face in the future.

When Granny Elephant of this era narrated all this, a baby elephant became very sad.

'What kind of troubles was the baby tusker going to face that the Granny Elephant of that time should have wept?' she asked the Granny Elephant of this era.

When the Granny Elephant of this era recalled the tragedies the baby tusker had to suffer, her eyes too brimmed with tears.

SIX

A Gift for Thithimol

The troubles began for the little tusker when he turned twenty years old. It all happened in our land, the land where there are stone quarries, saw mills, gunsmiths and blasting powder. Mannupaara Subin was the richest man in the area.

Mannupaara was not his family name. It was a moniker given to him by the public because he dealt in *mannu* [sand] and *paara* [granite]. Around the time we are talking of, suddenly a thought came to Subin: why don't I get married! From the moment the thought occurred to him, he could not sit, stand, lie down, walk or run. When he sat, he wanted to stand; when he stood up, he wanted to lie down; when he lay down, he wanted to run; when he ran, he wanted to walk. He was in a lather over the idea.

The idea of marrying entered his mind when he came across Thithimol, the most beautiful girl and the unrivalled braggart of that land. Subin conveyed his wish to her, but she brushed him aside. Finally, it was her friend who told Subin the secret.

'Man, you won't be able to marry her just like that. You will have to give her a gift to bring her around.'

'Is that all? What does she want as a gift? A car? A diamond necklace? A world tour? Let me know now and it will be delivered tomorrow,' Subin assured her.

'Aiyye, nothing corny like that. They are things that anyone who has money can buy for her. It must be a gift that no one else can give. First you find something like that. Then organise to get it. The rest we shall see later.'

This sent Mannupaara Subin into a tizzy. Was there such a thing? He had to find it. In the days that followed, he started to urgently look for such a gift, leaving every other work unattended.

When you have all the money, what can't you buy? On top of that, it must be unique. This was a big conundrum. When one thinks along these lines, marriage itself is a conundrum. However, one can't escape from marrying, can one?

Mannupaara Subin's stress levels went up. Once he got tense, he had this condition that made his limbs tremble. To control that, he was advised to eat wild buffalo meat.

Shivering all over, Subin headed straight to Gunner Chandy's home. That was one place where he could get wild buffalo meat. But when he reached there, there wasn't even a strip of wild buffalo meat in Chandy's home.

To get rid of Subin's shivering, Chandy gave him ground hibiscus flowers mixed in tender coconut water. However, when Subin drank it, his shivering increased.

'Son Subin, why are you shivering like this?' Chandy asked, as he watched the chair itself shake.

'Because of worry and tension, Chandy-chetta,' Subin said, still shivering on the chair.

'Why do you have so many worries?' Chandy wasn't ready to let go.

'You see, I have to give a gift to Thithimol. Something that no one else can give.' He managed to say shyly.

'Oh, you want to marry her?' His question received only an embarrassed nod from Subin in reply.

Then Subin asked, 'Chandy-chetta, can you think of such a gift?'

Although he replied 'In my knowledge there's no such thing', Chandy racked his brains to think of something that qualified.

Why? Because Subin had pots of money. If he delivered such a gift, Subin would reward him with a sackful of money.

It was a wedding. When Chandy wondered what could be an appropriate wedding gift, what came to his mind was the most beautiful married life he had seen.

Not only among the marriages he had seen, but among the ones that the whole world had witnessed.

'Shucks, what gift could he have given?' Gunner Chandy asked himself aloud.

'Who had given whom, chetta?' Subin was all agog.

'Oh, they are not people, they are elephants. I was wondering what gift Peacock Plume Tusker would have given his wife Leaf-ear on their wedding?'

'Peacock Plume Tusker?'

'Yes, there's a tusker in our forest. Not only me, no one would have seen tusks bigger and more beautiful than his. His tusks are not white. When those tusks catch the sun, they reflect the colours of a peacock's feathers. There is no better sight than that in the world. That's why he's called Peacock Plume Tusker.'

'That's interesting!' A few thoughts flitted through Subin's mind and he suddenly asked, 'Can I get those tusks, Chandy-chetta?'

'Aiyyo, Subin. That doesn't look possible. The mooppans claim he's no ordinary elephant.'

What the mooppans—the local tribal chieftains—had said was true. After all, wasn't Peacock Plume Tusker the miraculous elephant who was filled with Elephantam that had come down from the heavens. He was born in springtime. He grew up receiving love from all the elephants of that forest and the neighbouring ones too. He not only received their love, but he also returned it, multiplying it many times over.

As a result, though they were of an unseen beauty, none of the elephants cast an evil eye on his stunning tusks, which kept growing as a manifestation of pure, resplendent Elephantam.

Although all the elephants were his friends, the closest to him was Leaf-ear. They had become friends one morning, at a time when the mist lingered till the sun rose well above the trees. The Peacock Plume Tusker and Leaf-ear, they would amble along, engrossed in each other.

Through the grassy knolls where spotted deer and wild goats grazed; through the clear streams where striped carp chased their girlfriends to nudge and nuzzle; beneath the tree on which giant squirrels cracked open myrobalan fruits and shared the sweet kernels; along the bamboo forests where crickets, their wings folded, made undulating music for their friends—both of them used to saunter leisurely.

Two years after they got together, a baby tusker was born to them. When this baby's tusks grew and they flashed like lightning, everyone started to call him Lightning Tusker.

Lightning Tusker was four years old when Subin took a shine to Thithimol and turned up at Gunner Chandy's doorstep, hands and legs shivering.

When Subin asked him if the tusks were attainable, Chandy-chettan had surely replied they were not. Then Subin said this:

'Chandy-chetta, from what I have heard, those tusks can't be taken by anyone else in the world. Tusks having peacock feather colours! There is no better gift I could give Thithimol.'

'That's true. But, Subin, it isn't easy at all,' Chandy-chettan conveyed the near-impossibility of it happening.

'I know it is no small thing. But you can name your price. After that, if you think you'll need more, you can ask for more. Think about it, Chandy-chetta.'

Chandy was possessed by Misophantam since that instant. Misophantam would ensure that any hope of winning some money wouldn't stop at just hoping; it would continue to dog the person till the money was pocketed.

Thus, Gunner Chandy decided to wrest away the Elephantam tusks of Peacock Plume Tusker, father to Lightning Tusker.

It was wintertime. Mist would descend on the forest even before the onset of dusk. Peacock Plume Tusker and Leaf-ear still travelled together. Little Lightning Tusker would be trotting within beckoning distance.

For a month, Gunner Chandy tailed Peacock Plume Tusker. But whenever he got close enough, something or the other hindered him. Once a snake accosted and tried to bite him. It was a narrow escape.

Another time, when he drew the bead and was about to shoot, a clap of thunder startled him and made him miss his mark. Tripping over forest vines, sudden blindness, slipping and falling, leech bites, unexplained itches ... hindrances were endless. He started to feel that even if he were offered crores of rupees, he could do without the tusks.

However, greed makes people commit many sins. Misophantam would be in tow, aiding and abetting. Which was why the day arrived when Gunner Chandy's wickedness would succeed.

There was still some time before sunset. For two days, Gunner Chandy had been sitting still on a big rock. A little away from the rock was a tilia tree, filled with tender leaves. Around dusk was the time when its bark would be the tastiest.

The tilia bark was a delicacy that bull elephants fed their mates. Gunner Chandy was certain that Peacock Plume Tusker would turn up to tear off the sweet bark to present to Leaf-ear.

To use as projectiles in place of the metal rounds used as bullets in country guns, Chandy had brought four-inch spikes made from twisted rebars. His elephant gun was loaded with one of them. His hunch was correct. Peacock Plume Tusker and Leaf-ear waddled towards the tree, nuzzling and rubbing against each other. Baby Lightning Tusker was with them. But he did not go towards the tilia tree. He was busy trying to get at the tender fronds of a wild coconut tree nearby.

When the jumbo started to tear off the bark, Chandy lifted his elephant gun and let off a booming shot.

Misophantam whizzed and tore into Peacock Plume Tusker's brain.

Only when her mate went down with loud trumpeting did Leaf-ear realise the danger they were in. Though she was horrified, without leaving the side of her beloved, she tried to help him up. The terrified Lighting Tusker hid himself in a cluster of wild coconut trees. However, he could still see his father convulsing in death throes.

Gunner Chandy realised that in order to get to the tusks he had to drive Leaf-ear away from the fallen tusker. Misophantam came to his help again and gave him a wicked idea. Set the forest on fire!

Gunner Chandy decanted some petrol from the tank of a mechanical saw, poured it on some rags and threw them into the undergrowth. Then he struck his lighter and set the cloth on fire.

The sight of fire made Lightning Tusker bawl in terror. His cries brought Leaf-ear running to him. When he saw that she had moved away from Peacock Plume Tusker, Chandy started the mechanical saw. Lifting and carrying it, he walked towards the tusker.

Since she did not have the heart to watch what was to happen next and the fire was catching on, Leaf-ear gathered her son and beat a hasty exit ...

It was when, trapped inside the corral, he heard the terrifying sound of the saw once again that Lightning Tusker fully regained his consciousness.

Outside, the wardens were cutting wood to strengthen the stockade. Lightning Tusker looked at them with blazing eyes.

SEVEN

The Roving Search Squad

'Elephant herds have been seen lurking near the corral. Which is why we are strengthening it,' Hook Moustache boasted to the pressmen who had come to see Lightning Tusker. 'We know exactly how to handle each animal. Though the weather was against us the last two days, things were done as planned.'

'Was this guy so troublesome?' a journalist asked.

'Absolutely the biggest troublemaker of this forest. He has knocked down many houses. Trampled on crops. Killed three people.'

'Can you say "killed"? Weren't they killed in a stampede while trying to scare elephants with firecrackers?'

'Whatever it maybe, we lost the men, didn't we? We can now assure you that from now on there will be no elephant trouble. Let the people here sleep peacefully at night.'

Hook Moustache brought down the curtains on his bravado only after striking a few poses for the local TV channel's cameraman. Then he inspected again the sturdiness of the reinforcements.

'Super. Now even if a dinosaur comes and headbutts it, it won't move.' A smile broke out on his lips when he thought of the ease with which this mission had been accomplished. The smile turned into a leer, and as he stood there leering, darkness rolled in and it was soon night.

Whether it was because it was cloudy or for some other reason, it was a very dark night. The forest was rather silent. Hook Moustache felt it was a shame that there was nothing exciting happening.

The moment he felt so, came a hooting sound *gumm ... gumm ... gumm ...* Which bird hoots in this fashion? Is it not a bird? How come you are a forest officer and you don't know such things?

He started to feel a certain dread. But then it occurred to him that Lightning Tusker was inside the corral, so there was nothing to be worried about. It was when courage and hubris started to overflow in him that he left for the guesthouse to sleep.

It made no difference to the night if the ranger was keeping vigil or sleeping inside the building. It stayed as menacing as it was before.

About ten or fifteen kilometres away from the guesthouse, someone was restarting his work, which had been halted for some months. Moonshiner Manichandran. He was among the happiest persons to hear the news of Lightning Tusker's capture.

When Lightning Tusker was at large, he could not leave the wash, which was distilled to make hooch, out in the open. However remote a place he chose to mix the wash at, Lightning would sniff it out and reach there. The next morning, all that would be left were broken pots and drums. All the wash would have been drunk by the tusker.

Denied moonshine-making as a means of livelihood, Manichandran decided to earn a living by working as a manual labourer. That was when news of Lightning being captured reached him.

So, he thought—okay, back to moonshine! He gathered some black jaggery, rotting fruits and wheat, and mixed them in water to make the wash. Since sal ammoniac had been added liberally, by the time it was night, the wash frothed and gave off the distinctive smell.

'Let the smell spread through the forest. Lightning's in the cage. Nothing to worry about!'

A little away from the riverside where he had kept the wash, on top of a rock he built a small fire and went to sleep by its side.

Although he had thought it was a peaceful night with nothing to fear, if he had woken up and taken a look,

the sight would have frightened the living daylights out of him.

The moon was behind the clouds, so it was an inky-black night. No breeze to stir even a leaf. Add to that the cries and howls of different animals.

Unaware of all this, Manichandran was enjoying his sleep. But he did have to wake up. *Bim-bam, clatter-platter, clink-clonk* … a wild uproar woke him up.

As soon as he woke up, he shined the torch in the direction of the wash.

The blue plastic barrel in which the wash was kept had been trampled on and torn up. All the palm fronds kept around it as camouflage had been flung around. Pots and buckets kept near the barrel had been kicked and sent in all directions.

Letting out a terrified 'Aiyyo', Manichandran shone the torch all around him.

He caught a glimpse of Lightning disappearing into the forest, trampling underfoot the reed thickets near the riverbank. He saw only the elephant's rear as it lurched from side to side with all the wash sloshing inside it.

The sight made him decide that further outcry was uncalled for. Not that he could have screamed or shrieked in moderation or hysterically even if he wanted to. Fear ensured that not a peep came out of him.

'That's why I had said you won't be able to tie him down. He'll be there, he'll be here, he'll be everywhere. He can cloak and fade; knows black magic and voodoo,' said Chembaran Mooppan the next day to a wailing Manichandran and a flabbergasted Hook Moustache.

'Mooppa, this is the twenty-first century. Voodoo and black magic? Superstitions? Are you serious? We'll do one thing. Tonight, let the department's jeeps rove all over the forest. We should unearth the truth.'

It's possible that the moon wanted to make things easier for the search parties. There was bright moonlight that night. Three jeeps drove at a crawl along the road bordering the forest. High-power searchlights, powerful enough to light the whole world, had been fixed to the roofs of the jeeps.

Seven or eight wild boars that had come down the forest to eat the colocasia growing in Kunjandipanikkan's yard landed up in front of the second jeep.

'Who the hell is trying to shine light into our eyes?' lisped the mother boar as her overgrown tusks interfered with her speech. She stopped in front of the jeep and shouted a few fruity abuses. Those seated in the jeep laughed at her and kept driving.

At midnight, when she saw sun-like brightness flash through the window, the bedridden Elisha-chedathi jumped out of bed, crossed herself and whispered, 'It's the Second Coming, it's the Second Coming ...'

Butcher Joy sold pork from domestic Coorgi pigs as wild boar meat, leaving the hair on the skin unshaven. He also appeared in front of the search jeeps, his scooter loaded with two sackfuls of pork.

'Halt!' shouted the wardens and leapt out of the jeeps. They bodily lifted him and his scooter and took them to the forest office.

'You imbeciles, you have been sent out to corner the elephant, not to arrest this guy!' Hook Moustache was furious.

The search jeeps resumed their crawl, deciding not to get distracted.

An hour past midnight, the third jeep was parked by its driver near Buffalo Junction.

'We'll resume patrolling after sleeping for a little while,' one of the wardens said.

'Right-ho, it's enough to leave the lights on,' concurred the driver.

Turning one each of the searchlights in the four directions, everyone inside the jeep went to sleep. Maybe an hour would have passed. Suddenly the light directed towards the left side of the jeep burst with a *clink-clank* sound. Also, a stone the size of a healthy laddoo landed on a sleeping warden's chest. All the wardens woke up and jumped out of the jeep.

At no one in particular, they shouted and gesticulated, 'Who? What? Halt right now!' In the same instant, the next stone arrived. It was as big as a baby elephant. It fell on the jeep, breaking its back. The other searchlights were smashed and the jeep's roof crumpled and caved in.

The wardens did not wait to see further ballistics.

They ran screaming, 'Aiyyo, save us ... we are under attack!' One of them who wasn't able to run saw the jeep slowly rising up.

When he saw the rump of the elephant as it walked away with the jeep held up in the air, he mumbled, 'Lightning Tusker!'

The next morning, in front of the corral, facing the rear of Lightning Tusker, he gave witness.

'I saw it whole, I saw it all. All the wrinkles and folds and marks on the back, the curve at the tip of the tail ... same ... same ... like this one. He is him. Him is he.'

When the warden had completed his statement, Lightning Tusker turned around and gave him a look.

Terror-stricken by that look, the warden fell to his knees, touched his forehead to the ground and started to plead, 'Aiyyo, I haven't said anything, don't punish me ...'

'Is it because he's blessed by Elephantam that he's able to do all this?' one of the baby elephants asked Granny Elephant as she stood on the hilltop.

Granny chuckled and said, 'Who told you *he* did all that? Whether before he was captured or after, none of these acts is his doing.'

'Then who else is doing all this?' The baby elephants were amazed.

'It's him. He who lives in the forest invisible even to us.'

EIGHT

The Transformation of the *Mozha*

'You think we are sitting on our hands, doing nothing? Is it a goat or cow that we can tether on a whim? It's a wild elephant, no less. Give us some more time. We'll rest only after making you all feel secure.'

Hook Moustache spoke unconvincingly to the crowd of people clamouring in front of the forest office. The public refused to pipe down. They kept shouting and griping. They demanded that Lightning Tusker be shot and killed inside the corral immediately. A couple of them also flung stones at the corral.

Unmindful of the ruckus outside his corral, Lightning stood gazing at the forest faraway. He then let out a trumpet loud enough for the sound to carry to the heart of the forest.

The shock from the trumpet sent the crowd in front of the corral scattering in all directions. However, Lightning had no time for them. Within himself, he saw a rogue elephant walking through the pitch-darkness of the deep jungle.

When she heard the trumpeting, Granny said looking in the direction of the corral, 'He is calling out to his younger brother.'

'Younger brother? Does Lightning mama have a brother?' asked the baby elephants.

'Of course. Weren't the mother elephant and son elephant watching when the man killed Lightning's father, cut off his tusks and set the forest on fire? Lightning's mother Leaf-ear was pregnant at the time.'

The baby elephants huddled around Granny Elephant to hear the story. In that story, Leaf-ear and Lightning Tusker were scared of everything.

Wherever they would be, if the smell of humans, carried by the breeze, reached them, they used to run in the opposite direction. The sound of a leaf falling was enough to make them tremble. When the warmth of the sun touched them, afraid that it was from a fire, they would rush into the river.

When Lightning was small, his mother would tell him, 'My son, your father used to say that you would grow into a magnificent tusker. But all I am praying for now is that you don't grow tusks.' Moreover, she also wished for the baby she was carrying to be born as a she-elephant, because humans hankered after tusks. They would leave alone elephants without tusks.

But whether a baby will be a male or a female is not decided by the mother. The baby inside Leaf-ear was a male. And since his mother went around like a scaredy cat, carrying him inside her, he too was afraid of everything. He curled up in his mother's womb, paying no attention to what was happening elsewhere. When it was time to deliver him, his mother chose a meadow without stones and stakes.

When it was time, the baby would not come out. He was afraid to come out of his mother's body. Leaf-ear was very worried.

A couple of days passed like that.

A minister and his family wanted to offer prayers at a temple. A helicopter was arranged in quick time. To reach the temple, the helicopter had to fly over the meadow which Leaf-ear had chosen to deliver her baby in.

When she heard the whirring of the helicopter coming from the valley, Leaf-ear got nervous. The buzz of the mechanical saw was uppermost in her mind.

When the helicopter was directly overhead, the minister's two grandchildren flying with him saw two elephants below them.

'Hurray, wow! Wild elephants,' they cheered.

Assuming that if he humoured the grandchildren, he would get into the good books of the minister, the pilot lowered the aircraft. Leaf-ear and her companion started to run across the meadow when they saw the helicopter headed towards them.

When he realised that his mother was running for her life on a juddering run, the baby tusker too felt the fright. He started to spin around in the womb. That made him pop out of his mother's womb.

'Wow, we saw a wild elephant calving,' the minister exulted. He also decided that the helicopter's pilot, who made it possible for them to see the elephants, should be suitably rewarded.

Trembling with fear, when he emerged from his mother's womb and heard the whirring of the helicopter, the baby elephant was as good as dead. He curled up right where he had fallen out of his mother's body and lay still.

Normally, elephant calves, as soon as they drop, struggle to their feet, wobble and go and drink their mother's milk. Wondering why this baby wasn't doing that, Leaf-ear nudged him with her foot, sending him rolling. He rolled to the side and showed no signs of getting up.

Though she felt sorry that he wasn't getting to his feet, she also felt somewhat relieved. Her baby was not a she-elephant as she had hoped. Rather than him growing up to provide humans with ivory, wasn't it better that he was stillborn?

The tearful mother and her female companion pondered on what was to be done next. Finally, they decided to abandon the unmoving calf in the meadow and leave.

Leaf-ear walked up to her son. She caressed his body gently with her trunk.

After the helicopter had gone away, taking its howling sound with it, the baby elephant's fright receded. However, when he thought he had come to a place he knew nothing of, he did not feel like opening his eyes.

In that instant, disobeying its mother, an impish grasshopper urchin ran out of a clump of grass and started its exploration of the world. To be honest, grasshoppers don't run, they spring. Springing and leaping, it reached where the baby elephant lay.

'Mother of God, what's this thing?'

For the first time it was seeing something that was balled up in that fashion. Initially it was a little nervous. But not for long. The reckless madcap started to bounce on it, having decided to find out what this thing really was.

The grasshopper urchin's bouncing all over him was of no concern to the baby elephant lying with his eyes tightly shut. He just lay there, slumbering.

Only when it got on top of the baby elephant did the grasshopper urchin realise its blunder. Being a calf delivered only a few minutes ago, his body was covered in a sticky, oozy substance. Not only was the urchin slipping all over the place, the gooey stuff began to stick to its body too. It needed to wipe that off.

With great effort, it managed to leap off the baby elephant's body, and landed on the tip of a citronella leafstalk.

That tip held a bud that, much to its disappointment, wasn't able to bloom despite much straining because its sepals were too tough. The grasshopper urchin, having landed with its sticky feet, thrashed and yanked vigorously to free itself. As a result, two of the bud's sepals tore off, and the flower bloomed and spread its fragrance.

As the urchin stood wailing with the sepals stuck to its feet, its mother arrived, scolded it and then pushed and prodded it so that it fell back into the grass.

The leafstalk was very close to the tip of the baby elephant's trunk. Without taking permission from anyone around, the flower's fragrance entered the baby elephant's nostrils. When that smell reached his brain, he opened his eyes without intending to.

His eyes first fell on his mother who stood nuzzling him with her trunk. When she saw him opening his eyes, she felt happy at first. She helped him stand, propping him up with her trunk. When he rose and looked around, an unnamed fear gripped him.

He grew up timid. He was always found walking between his mother's legs. Even when Leaf-ear stopped nursing him, he continued to cling to her teats. By that time, his elder brother Lightning had grown into an imposing tusker with a broad head and exquisite tusks.

One day, he approached his little brother who was still hiding between his mother's four legs.

'Baby brother, come, let's play in the mud,' he invited. Since he loved his big brother, the little one came out slowly. He kept rubbing against his big brother's leg as they walked down to the marsh at the foot of the hill.

Baby elephants were frolicking and somersaulting in the slushy mud.

'Your baby sister is very shy, dear fellow,' one of his friends said to Lightning.

'Aiyyo, not my sister—my younger brother,' Lightning corrected him.

'Huh? Brother? In that case, shouldn't there be at least one tiny tusk on him?' asked one of the baby elephants.

'That's true. You, his brother, have such huge tusks,' another one voiced his doubts.

'Yes, my mother said that your brother is a *mozha*. A tusker without tusks.' A silly baby elephant spilled whatever he had heard from his mother in front of everyone.

This made Lightning's little brother very sad. He ran back to his mother. His mother too chose to scold him.

'They say such things because of your nature. Instead of staying in my shadow all the time, why can't you go and play with them? If you stay here chomping on my teats, your tusks will never grow. You'll become a mozha.'

Leaf-ear had, of course, forgotten her wish that he should never grow tusks.

Hearing this from his own mother broke the little one's heart. He wanted to cry. But if he was seen weeping, everyone would mock him. He had to find a place where he could cry alone, away from prying eyes. He set off immediately in search of such a place.

That was the first time he was walking all by himself. His mother thought he had gone to meet Lightning. But he took a different route. That path led to a rocky terrain which elephants always avoided.

When he reached the cavernous rock formations, he got frightened by the darkness around him. He doubled up and leaned against a rock. Now he could cry to his heart's content.

After weeping and sniffling for a long time, the darkness around him began to seem like an elephant. A mozha without the tusks of light. The rocks also appeared to be elephants. He felt happy that he had won some new friends.

When dusk fell, he realised that he wasn't the only occupant of the cave. Giant bats were hanging down from the roof. As they set off for their nightly hunt, the sound of their flapping wings echoed through the caves and startled him.

Unable to remain there for another moment, the baby elephant came away, back to his mother. Although he had decided that he would never return to that cave, he did have to retrace his steps.

When his friends ridiculed him, calling him a mozha ...

When young she-elephants whispered among themselves, giving him sidelong glances, and jeered ...

When he witnessed all the elephants praising Lightning as he, flashing his tusks, drove away the tigers attacking the elephants ...

When he heard the mocking laughter of other tuskers as they, using their tusks, removed obstacles from the path of the elephant herd ...

on many such occasions, Tuskless Tusker had to head back to the dark cave.

When he talked to the darkness inside the cave, he felt a great sense of relief. After some time, he stopped talking to everyone, save this darkness.

Except for his trips to the cave, he went everywhere else with his mother. One day, he and his mother were walking down to the river at the foot of the hill. Suddenly three or four tender leaves fluttered down in front of them from a tree buffeted by the wind. The mother elephant looked up instinctively.

The tilia trees were covered in tender leaves. Old memories flooded her mind. She stepped aside from the path leading to the river and started to walk in between the trees, with Tuskless Tusker trotting alongside, rubbing against her legs.

They reached the old rock that had been witness to a tragedy. From the burnt-down stump of the tilia tree, another tilia tree had sprouted. Leaf-ear walked up to that tree and caressed it and the ground beneath it with her trunk.

Since he was in the habit of doing whatever his mother did, Tuskless Tusker too swept his trunk over the tree and the ground beneath it. And when his trunk swept the ground, suddenly he could smell his father, Peacock Plume Tusker, in the soil.

Next came the smell of burning. And then a throbbing sound which made his head feel as if it was being split into two. Someone was wailing. All this drove him crazy and he started rooting through the ground.

Leaf-ear was perturbed by the sight of her son's agitation. She called out to him to return to their path. But he did not heed the call. The crazed look in his eyes told her that he would never heed her call again.

Taken aback by the way his face and body had changed, the unnerved mother started to trudge back.

What Tuskless Tusker did next was something he had never done before. His trunk held high, he bellowed with all his strength.

It was powerful enough to set the human settlements and the forest trembling. Granny Elephant, who had heard many such elephant calls, said, 'The mozha has been possessed by Misophantam. Now he will run riot.'

NINE

Failcat Tiger

After leaving his mother, friends and other forest dwellers behind, Tuskless Tusker who had gone rogue came out only in the night. The mornings were spent in the cave, wrestling with the darkness, grappling with his trunk, making it bend over, punching the small of his back with it and flinging it against the cave walls.

In the night, he would emerge and pussyfoot without making a sound. He did not go far in search of food. He was happy with what was available nearby. By the time the bats returned from their forays into the hamlet, he too would be back in the cave.

It was an early morning, with a lazy, light drizzle. Though there was a suggestion of silver on the eastern horizon, the light was not strong enough to pierce the curtain of rain. Tuskless Tusker was returning after a visit to the neighbouring hill.

As soon as he entered the cave, he got a feline smell and stopped. Then he thought, *what the heck, let whoever wants to do whatever, it is not my lookout*, and made his way in.

The instant he went into the darkness, there was a roar and a leap. The performer of those acts truly wished it to be a blood-curdling roar and wished to smash the elephant's brain into mush with its paw.

But what did actually happen?

A plaintive bleat, a little louder than a cat's mew, and a futile leap far short of the elephant's head and a slide along the trunk.

'Don't move, I'll smash your head in one swipe,' the tiger said, clinging to the elephant for dear life and to avoid flopping down onto the cave floor.

The wheezy mew and the tickle on his trunk in the darkness had startled Tuskless Tusker a little. He shook his body slightly. The tiger was flung against the rocks of the cave.

'Girl, do you need to show your ferocity against a weakling like me, who can barely stand? Why don't you pick on someone of your size, for instance some elephant?' the tiger asked from among the rocks where he had fallen, his aggression down several notches.

The tuskless tusker sized up the tiger. Just a namesake tiger. An emaciated, skinny-buttocked creature on wobbly legs.

Still flat on his back, the tiger demanded, 'Girl, what's your plan? Are you going to let me lie like this, die and rot?'

'To let you die?' Tuskless Tusker could not understand what was going on.

'If you don't want me to die, help me up, girl. You pushed me down and now you stand over me as if you had nothing to do with it.'

When he heard that, Tuskless Tusker felt guilty as if he had committed some evil act.

'Please forgive me, grandpa.' The tuskless tusker respectfully helped the tiger on to his spindly legs.

'Whose grandpa are you talking of? Girl, I am still a tiger in the prime of his youth, do you understand? A *young* tiger! Which is why I decided that if I should hunt, I should hunt nothing lesser than an elephant,' the tiger spoke, leaning against a rock.

That made Tuskless Tusker laugh.

'Don't laugh. There's only one animal in the forest that has no equal. That is the elephant. I want the fame of having hunted down and captured a paragon among elephants.'

'In that case, my friend, you hunt my brother, Lightning Tusker. He's the paragon of elephants,' Tuskless Tusker said, his head bowed.

'You cunning girl, you still want to get me killed, don't you? If I had the power to hunt a tusker, wouldn't I have defeated that gutsy tiger and won the tigress's hand?

Stop joking.' The tiger managed to stand somewhat straight and talk. In between, though he tried to catch a rat that ran across the cave floor, he failed.

'You also want to defeat someone, don't you?' enquired Tuskless Tusker.

'Oh yes, among us tigers, if we need to get a tigress as a mate, we have to trounce the other tigers in the group. There was one whom all other tigers could trounce.'

'Who was that?' the elephant asked anxiously.

'Me. Who else? That's why I am now hiding from everyone. After hunting and bringing down an elephant, I will return! In glory! That day, all of them will stand before me like timid toddy cats, their heads bowed.'

'Assuming that will happen, I should be afraid to be with you,' Tuskless Tusker feigned fear.

'Yes, you should be afraid, very afraid. I don't understand you, girl. Why are you living in this dark hole and that too all alone? Which, of course, makes you land up in front of terrors like me.' The tiger tried to talk himself up once more and failed.

'I'm no girl, don't girl me. I am a he,' Tuskless Tusker said with irritation, fed up with being mistaken.

'Huh?' The tiger looked him up and down, round and around, here and there. After he had seen him from all possible angles, he still had doubts.

'Where are your tusks?'

'I live in this darkness all alone because of that,' Tuskless Tusker said ruefully.

'Aha, that's the reason,' the tiger said and tried to roar with laughter. What came out was a vanilla, run-of-the-mill laughter.

'So, in a way we are equals—in our sorrows. A tusker without tusks and a tiger without ferocity. Given we are so alike, I won't attack you. From now on, we shall move forward, hand in hand. Do you understand?'

The elephant did not respond. The tiger then looked around to assuage his hunger. The elephant did not pay any attention to the tiger shamelessly acting beneath his station—catching worms and cockroaches and chomping on them.

After a while, the tiger said, 'It's possible that everyone else in this world is trying to get us or cheat us. But why should we hide ourselves in this cave and starve? You know what's my way?'

'What's your way?'

'That's something you should learn. If I feel low, I go on a trip. That's when we understand something.'

'What do we understand?'

'That majority of the others in the world are bigger failures than us.'

'Really?'

'Of course! Go out and take a look, if you really want to understand the way things are.'

The tusker was reluctant. He wasn't able to move from where he stood. He was still being his old self.

Only when the tiger let fly a volley of old-style abuses did he agree to venture out with him.

The forest was bright and clear after the morning rain. Unable to open his eyes due to the brightness of the sunlight, the elephant stood for a while.

Then they heard a hammering noise.

'What's that?' the elephant asked.

'That? That's the crooked-tail woodpecker working on the tree.'

'Arrghhh ... such a racket. Why is he doing it?'

'Very true. Just imagine the state of his head. He's looking for food. See for yourself—what kind of poppycock will he get in return for all these troubles!'

The little tusker willed his eyes open, deciding this was one sight he had to see.

At first, everything was blurred. Slowly things became clearer.

The woodpecker was watching vainly as the hole became deeper with each peck. There was some creature inside the hole. To pull it out, the woodpecker kept pecking harder and deeper. When the hole was big enough, a snake that lay comfortably coiled inside poked its head out. Asking the woodpecker why it couldn't be left in peace, the snake began hurling abuses at it.

'Did you see—what did he get after all that head-wrenching pecking? He was humiliated at the end of it. That was all. Shall I tell you a truth?' The tiger looked at the elephant like only a teacher would.

'Tell me.'

'Really, the majority of the creatures in the world live a life of disgrace. To put it another way, to live in this world, one must be prepared to face humiliation. If you remain stuck to your useless pride and dignity, nothing's going to work.'

In the middle of this sermon, the tiger had caught some insect and swallowed it. They could hear the sounds of the woodpecker going *peck ... peck ... peck ...* at some other tree.

'That crooked-tail is at it again. Shameless fellow! You come with me.' The tiger strode ahead, bidding the elephant to join him.

They went up and down many hills. All the way, the tiger kept pointing out many sights to Tuskless Tusker.

When they reached beneath a tamarind tree, the leaves of which had closed and had turned down as if they were browbeaten by the torrid look the sun gave them, the tiger said, 'This is only a ruse. Look at them in the night. They will be standing up smartly like the rooster's tail feathers.'

Wherever they looked, they saw weaklings—the cuckoo chick pecked at by a murder of crows; monkeys whose leaps missed the branches; insects that acted 'poor-me!' and beseeched with folded hands to be let off when the tiger caught them.

'Do you think they are failures?'

Since the elephant did not seem to understand things, the tiger did not bother to explain further.

They were on top of a tall hill. From that point, they could see the human settlements below.

'Eda, Tuskless Tusker. We have nothing to lose. Shall we make a play?'

'Make a play for what?' The elephant did not get the drift.

'The fights among us animals of the forest are of no consequence. If we have to win, we need to win against, look, those guys who walk around so full of Misophantam! The worst and wickedest of all in the entire universe: HUMAN BEINGS!'

Failcat Tiger and Tuskless Tusker stood on the hill and gazed down at the hamlets below where the humans were bickering among themselves for no good reason.

'It's true. They are the ones who should be defeated.'

'If we go down and flatten them, we will not have any enemies in the forest. But to do that, Elephantam, tigerishness and all that are not enough. We need pure Misophantam! Eda Tuskless Tusker, that's what we need to become—the worst misophants: humans.'

TEN

Granny Sandalwood Tree

'This land should not have seen a more opulent wedding than my daughter's,' Mannupaara Subin said, sitting grandly on the mahogany chair in Gunner Chandy's home.

'If you have decided that's the way it should be, then that's how it will be.' Gunner Chandy had no doubts.

'Yeah, that's all there is to it. But Chandy-chetta, I can't find enough sandalwood,' Subin shared his worry.

'Why do you need so much sandalwood?'

'Because the bed should be made of sandalwood, the wardrobe should be made of sandalwood, the bridal trunk too. My daughter's wish! It's not just the furniture. The guests need to apply sandal paste on their forehead. The venue should have sandal incense. It's a sandal-themed wedding.' When he said that, Subin held his head high.

'Who decided all this?' Chandy asked.

'My daughter Gaja and her mother Thithimol. Aren't they past masters in this kind of showboating?' Subin gave a sardonic smile.

'Excellent theme. But this means you'll need the whole sandalwood tree that stands on Koorachi Hill.' Gunner Chandy said, after doing some mental arithmetic.

'Yeah, yeah, will need it. Will need it.' Subin nodded vigorously.

'But Subin, we need to watch the moon. We can cut it only on a new moon day.'

'Do as you wish, Chandy-chetta. We still have some days left for the wedding. I thought it prudent to tell you in advance.' Sealing the deal thus, Subin stood up and shook hands with Gunner Chandy.

On new moon day, a Tuesday, Gunner Chandy, accompanied by three woodcutters, climbed the hill with chainsaws and other implements, then trudged through meadows, vine forests and swamps, and finally reached the foot of Koorachi Hill.

More than ten thousand fireflies were flickering on the sandalwood tree, switching on and off to some unseen timer. Therefore, though it was pitch dark, Chandy-chettan and his gang could see the tree from the foot of the hill.

'Why's it that only the sandalwood tree has so many fireflies?' Gunner Chandy asked his workers.

'Boss, who knows what gobbledygook this is.' Though the worker who responded did not know the reason, everyone in the forest did.

Granny Sandalwood was always caressing every tree and plant growing on that hill with her roots that ran deep underground.

Moreover, Granny Sandalwood would hold conversations with, and ask to talk about themselves, every creature that walked, crawled or flew through the forest.

It was her birthday. Dear to everyone, the fireflies had come to garland her.

Failcat Tiger and Tuskless Tusker too decided to pay her a visit and were headed to Koorachi Hill.

Clueless about this, Gunner Chandy and his workers reached the sandalwood tree. They walked around her, assessing her in the light of their headlamps, as she stood swaying in the night breeze, her branches spread out.

The lethal-looking light of the headlamps caused the frightened fireflies to kill their own lights. They closed their wings and clung to Granny Sandalwood.

'There seems to be some problem there. Walk a little faster,' Failcat said when he saw the abrupt snuffing out of the fireflies.

'Boys, chop the branches first and bring them down. Don't waste a single twig.'

When they heard Chandy's instructions, the woodcutters clambered up Granny Sandalwood's trunk and started roping the branches.

Soon it was time to cut the branches. The chainsaw was switched on in the light of an emergency lamp.

As the buzz of the saw got louder, so did Misophantam in Chandy.

'Get on with it, you good-for-nothing guys. Cut and push them down!'

'Boss, I thought I heard the growl of a tiger,' one of the woodcutters expressed his misgivings.

'Ach, no! That is the growl of the tiger saw. Focus on your work!' Chandy's Misophantam was in the ascendant. The chainsaw wielder took the opportunity to move closer to the sandalwood tree. Suddenly a stone came flying and shattered the emergency lamp.

'Aiyyo, what was that?' asked a worker, switching his headlamp back on.

He swivelled around to look. But before his swivel was complete, he was up in the air. The others did not understand who had hung him like a cloth on a clothesline on the rope tied to the tree, or who had snatched the headlamp of another worker and flung it away. But Gunner Chandy did—he knew it was an elephant.

He and his workers did not know, however, where to clamber up or in which direction to flee. Like the darkness enveloping them, the elephant was at large and omnipresent. The chainsaw that had fallen from the hands of the worker was snarling *kkreeee ... krreee*.

The growl of a tiger could be heard above that sound. Chandy realised there was some truth in what his worker had said. Before he could be sure, he had a feeling that the chainsaw was moving towards him.

The worker who was hanging on to the rope to escape from hurtling down to the ground could only hear the sound of the chainsaw. Many things were happening beneath him. What they were would be known only when the day broke. He clutched the rope firmly.

* * * *

Subin was waiting for Gunner Chandy to deliver the sandalwood.

'Before you realise, the wedding day will be upon us. How come you are not showing any urgency on the matter of sandalwood?' Thithimol did not hide her displeasure and sounded cross.

'Will you pipe down a bit? Chandy-chettan has gone to get it. He'll deliver it on time.' Subin was as cool as a cucumber.

'One more thing. Gaja-mol now says she also wants the Peacock Plume's tusks in her dowry,' reported Thithimol.

'Do you agree with her? Wouldn't it be better if those tusks remained with us?' Though Gaja was his daughter, Subin did not like her greed.

'Then let her keep them at least for a few days. We can always have them back.'

'Ah, that we can do. Let her win some prestige in her husband's family.' Subin assented.

'If we send them as they are, it won't make a splash. We need to band them with gold.' Thithimol's vanity was leaping to the skies.

'If we need to band them, it must be done in utmost secrecy. Where can we do that?'

'If we take them to Ratheeshan, he will do it without a soul knowing about it.' Thithimol had a solution too.

Subin decided to take the tusks to Ratheeshan the next day itself. It had to be done without anyone knowing about it and he couldn't take anyone's help. When night fell, he loaded the tusks in the back of his van and left for Ratheeshan's smithy.

* * * *

'We did nothing. The chainsaw they themselves had brought did it to them, that's all,' Failcat told Tuskless Tusker as he stood with his head bowed.

'Breaking the lights and flinging the worker on to the rope, all that we did, right?' Tuskless Tusker asked in all honesty.

'What, should we let the men who had come to cut down Granny Sandalwood go scot-free? Boy, you need to learn a lot of things. Only then will you become a real tusker.' Failcat had given that advice offhandedly. He was busy with other thoughts. All of that came out in the form of a question.

'Let me ask you something. Does this jackfruit that you are going to eat now taste like venison?'

'For us elephants, jackfruit is tastier than venison.'

'I see. In that case, I must try it,' Failcat said gravely.

Tuskless Tusker found this odd. 'Do tigers eat jackfruit?'

'One must eat something to stay alive, old chap.' Dropping his solemn expression, Failcat broke into tears and started to bawl.

'Shush ... don't cry, my friend, don't ... What if someone sees you?' Tuskless Tusker said, holding him close with his trunk.

Failcat continued to bawl. To cheer him up, Tuskless Tusker said, 'This jackfruit orchard that we are walking through, do you know why it was planted?'

'I don't know.' Failcat was still crying.

'There is a goat pen at the end of this orchard. The trees were planted to feed jackfruit leaves to the goats.'

To check if this had piqued Failcat's curiosity, Tuskless Tusker watched him closely.

Failcat was indignant. 'What use to me is a goat inside a pen?'

'Can't an elephant smash a goat pen if he feels like it—' Before Tuskless Tusker could complete the sentence, Failcat had leapt up and planted a kiss on his cheek.

'Walk a little faster, dear boy,' Failcat said, settling down on top of the elephant.

Two hillocks beyond Ponnappan's jackfruit orchard was Ratheeshan's house. With the thrill of reaching his destination, Subin drove the van towards the yard with the engine roaring.

Something in the vehicle's headlights suddenly caught Subin's eye. A thick vine was hanging down from one of the trees by the roadside. He drove on, taking it for an ordinary vine. But then he had a doubt—that did not look like an ordinary vine.

He reversed the van and looked carefully at the vine. It was a tiger's tail! Suddenly Misophantam frothed up inside him.

He reversed the van a little further and got hold of his gun. Strapping on his headlamp, he switched it on and stepped out of the van.

It was indeed a tiger. Subin leaned against the van and took aim. A stone came whizzing out of the blue and smashed his headlamp. A startled Subin began to shoot aimlessly. But the shots hit nothing. Venting his frustration, he thumped the van's body a couple of times.

At first, he thought the van had taken offence to being thumped and was retaliating. But then he saw that the van had done a somersault and was hurtling straight towards his head.

As he was turning away from the upturned vehicle, Tuskless Tusker heard a bellow that no one else heard. An elephant bellow that hurt the listener. He had heard this bellow earlier too, along with the growl of a chainsaw, many years ago.

Tuskless Tusker could see some rays coming from the van, something other than light. He was arrested by the power of Elephantam and turned back.

'Friend, is there something in that van?'

'Yeah, bilge water! Who the hell asked you to create a ruckus by overturning the van before I could catch a goat?' Failcat was livid.

'I need to know what it is.' Ignoring Failcat, Tuskless Tusker started to pummel the van to break it open. By then the forest wardens and their jeeps could be seen heading in their direction.

'Oh boy, the whole platoon is coming! Let's make good our escape now,' Failcat tried to hustle him.

Tuskless Tusker pulled out a box from inside the smashed-up van and threw it down. It broke into pieces.

Inside it were two huge rainbow-coloured tusks that gleamed even before the light from the approaching forest department jeeps could hit them.

Until Failcat bit on his tail and started to drag him away, Tuskless Tusk stood staring at those tusks.

ELEVEN

Rainbow Tusks

'The rainbow tusks that forest wardens had retrieved from Subin's wrecked van that night are still there,' Granny Elephant told the baby elephants.

'Where?' one of the babies asked.

'In the forest office by the side of the corral where Lightning mama is kept.'

'Doesn't Tuskless Tusker know this?'

'Absolutely. Aren't those tusks pure Elephantam? And aren't the two brothers the sons of Peacock Plume Tusker?' said another little elephant.

'But what's the use? One brother is being held by men in a cage; and the other slinks away in the forest,' commented one of the baby elephants who did not fully understand the power of Elephantam.

'Umm, for now it is so. But my children, we know nothing about the power of Elephantam. Who knows what all it's going to do!'

Granny stopped talking and walked into the deep forest with the baby elephants in tow. Suddenly a strong wind sprang up out of nowhere. The baby elephants got a fright. They trotted behind Granny.

When the wind blew down the valley and up the hills, meandered through the forest and finally reached Tuskless Tusker who was standing but in deep sleep inside the dark cave, it woke him up. He looked around.

Why this sudden gust of wind? It seemed to be bearing some tidings.

'What is this, my friend?' he asked Failcat, who lay curled up on a rock.

'Nicely rotting meat of a buffalo's rump,' said Failcat, in the midst of his dream.

'What buffalo? All you can think about is food, nothing else?' The elephant struck Failcat with his trunk.

As he tumbled down from the rock, Failcat could not control his grief.

'What is this, old chap! I get something to eat only in my dreams. You won't let me do even that in peace? What do you want to know?'

'What is inside that wind?'

'What wind?'

'Pay attention. Isn't there a plaintive cry in this wind that's circulating inside the cave?'

Failcat cocked his ears and tried to listen intently.

'There's some sound. Can't say it's plaintive or cry or anything.'

'Let's go out and check.'

Tuskless Tusker stepped out without waiting for Failcat. Since he was habituated to walking along with the elephant, Failcat also emerged from the cave. When the elephant stepped on the rocks outside the cave and started to climb up, the wind became stronger.

When he reached the hilltop from where the whole forest could be seen, he felt as if the wind had stopped. Yet, he stood there as if waiting for something.

'Are you in *musth*?' Failcat asked him.

'Why?' The elephant was gazing into the distance.

'Nothing. I see a lot of changes in you. That's why I thought so. That was such a good sleep I was having.' Failcat prepared to curl up on a rock there.

Just then, the wind that Tuskless Tusker was waiting for reached them. The plaintive cry in it was very distinct.

'My brother …' Recognising his brother's voice, Tuskless Tusker said, looking in the direction of the corral in which Lightning Tusker was being held captive.

'Who?' Failcat asked.

'My brother Lightning Tusker is crying. What has happened to him?'

'You should go and ask Granny Elephant. She's the one who wanders all over the forest.'

'That's not possible. I don't want to go anywhere near the herd.' Tuskless Tusker turned around.

'Old chap, what kind of a decision is that?'

'Everyone in the herd ridiculed me. They called me a mozha. Apparently, this tuskless me wasn't good enough to be part of the herd.'

When he heard that, Failcat started to chortle, then guffawed, then, slapping on the rock, belly-laughed, then rolled on the floor, laughing.

'What the hell are you laughing for?' Tuskless Tusker was starting to get angry.

'Who said that you are a mozha? In all my wanderings all these years, I am yet to meet a tusker as courageous, valorous and imperious as you. Who can stand up to you? So if you tell me now that you will go hide in the cave, what else will I do but laugh?'

'Then why did they mock me?'

'Immaturity, what else? Those who don't believe in themselves find faults in others and mock them. If you have any doubts, you go and confront them. If you do that, any tusker will go weak in the knees out of fear.'

When he heard that, Tuskless Tusker lifted his head.

'If that be so, I need to prove myself, not to anyone else but to myself.' Tuskless Tusker looked at Failcat with a new self-assurance.

'I think the time has come. Why is your brother crying?' Failcat dropped his jocular attitude.

'He needs help. But what can I do alone?' Tuskless Tusker looked at Failcat.

'Why do you need to walk alone? Old chap, my mother would tell me, learn from the elephants.

For everything, you all set out together like the humans do. If you work together, is anything impossible? Go, call all the elephants, gather them together. Then defeat the humans. I will be with you, if you need me. My reputation too will improve. The reputation of having defeated humans.'

Tuskless Tusker stood looking at Failcat for a little while. For the first time, he felt a warm admiration for Failcat. He caught him in his trunk and lifted him bodily onto his head. Failcat managed to seat himself without slipping down. He felt as if he was an army commander! He screamed at the top of his voice, 'Go! Go to Granny Elephant the soonest you can.'

Tired from walking all day and from the anxieties about Lightning's condition, Granny Elephant was slumbering, leaning against a rock. Once she fell asleep, her snores were heard throughout the forest … *tttrrro … ttrrrrooo* … Other elephants gave her a wide berth.

'What snoring! How are the other elephants tolerating this oldie?' Failcat asked from his seat atop Tuskless Tusker, who was hiding himself behind a tree.

'We shall come later, let her wake up,' Tuskless Tusker turned around.

'Old chap, this is an emergency, how can you leave just like that?' Failcat reminded him.

Although she was in deep sleep, when Tuskless Tusker had reached her, so had his smell. When she realised that after the passage of so many years he had returned to the herd, she was very happy. However, she stood as if still asleep. Someone else should have welcomed him back into the fold.

'Son ...' The call came from among the leaves like falling rain.

Tuskless Tusker stopped in his tracks. An immeasurable anguish marked this voice that he had last heard many years ago beneath the tilia tree.

'Who called out for you?' asked Failcat.

'My mother.' There was a crack in Tuskless Tusker's voice.

'Son, why are you hiding there? Come here.' When they heard Granny Elephant bidding like that, all the other elephants looked around. They had not seen the elephant hiding behind the tree.

'Come son, we have all been waiting for you,' Granny opened her eyes and said.

Tuskless Tusker emerged from behind the tree, with Failcat seated on top of him. To the eyes of the other elephants, with his height, imperious bearing and the tiger seated atop him, Tuskless Tusker appeared to be an elephant god who had descended from another world.

His mother alone walked up to him and started to caress his trunk. Like in old times, Tuskless Tusker moved closer to her and stood rubbing himself against her legs.

Watching the scene, as he climbed down and leapt on to a rock, Failcat mocked, 'Cho chweet ... such a baby.'

The herd were dumbstruck by the vision of Tuskless Tusker in their presence. For his part, Tuskless Tusker was pleased as he watched the elephants who had mocked him now stand in awe before him. But the glee vanished as soon as he remembered his brother's cries.

'Mother, I heard Lightning's cry for help. What happened to him?'

When she heard that question, Granny was happy. 'So you have come for that!'

Granny told him how Dr Tharappan had shot Lightning with tranquilisers claiming that he had attacked humans, and how the forest wardens had captured and chained him in the corral near the forest office.

'But it was I who had attacked the humans. What has my brother got to do with it, why is he in the stockade?'

'They want his tusks. He has been kept in captivity for his tusks. He will not live much longer.'

When he heard Granny's words, Tuskless Tusker was enraged; he lifted his trunk and bellowed deafeningly. The whole forest trembled at the sound. All the elephants bowed their heads worshipfully before Tuskless Tusker.

'Mother, gran, friends … before this night is over, my brother Lightning will be freed.' His voice was firm and filled with grit.

As soon as he said that, he turned around and started to walk.

Granny looked at his gait and said proudly, 'That's the walk of someone who's going to redeem Elephantam.'

Next came a command from the matriarch: 'This is not his fight alone. All the elephants of this forest must join him.'

Hearing the din that was shaking up the entire forest, the tigress woke up with a start. When she looked around, the sight that met her eyes startled her more.

Riding a mammoth elephant was her suitor who had fled from the forest after losing to the other tigers. Now he was leading an army of elephants to some unknown war! Was he so brave? She thought that was interesting, and it opened a new line of thought.

'Tiger bhai …' she called out to see the reaction. Although when he heard the call, Failcat wanted to leap down and run to her with a 'yes, darling', he reined in the impulse and continued to sit regally atop the leading elephant.

Watching him as he passed by without so much as a glance at her, the tigress blinked and her jaw dropped to the floor.

'Get out of the way, you scaredy cat!'

The tiger who was preening himself looking at his image in the forest stream on his way to paying his third wife a visit was shocked by this snarling warning from another tiger. When he looked up, he saw Failcat seated on the tallest elephant he had seen and leading the elephant army.

'Eda, let me finish this mission and get back. Will teach you a lesson then!' As if the sight weren't enough, when he heard that too being said, the gutsy tiger lost his nerves.

He escaped narrowly from being trampled on by the elephant army as they stomped through the forest stream sending the water spraying in all directions.

Since by then he had realised that the elephant inside the corral could bring more trouble to his door, Hook Moustache had erected more fortifications and strengthened his defences.

Blinding floodlights were placed all around the forest office and corral, turning night into day. The number of guards posted there had increased manifold. Another ring of rail fences and timber walls too had been built around the plot on which the forest office stood.

After making all these arrangements and dropping a paan into his mouth, Hook Moustache sat down in his office, ready to keep awake through the night. By the time it was midnight, some of the guards had started to nod off. When the nodding turned into deep sleep, one of the guards started to feel the need to pee. The urge became urgent and that woke him up.

As soon as he got up, he started to pee without minding whoever may be watching. Suddenly, he was assailed by elephant smell.

He thought it came from Lightning Tusker. But when the smell spread everywhere and became strong enough to stir other sleepers, he realised something was amiss.

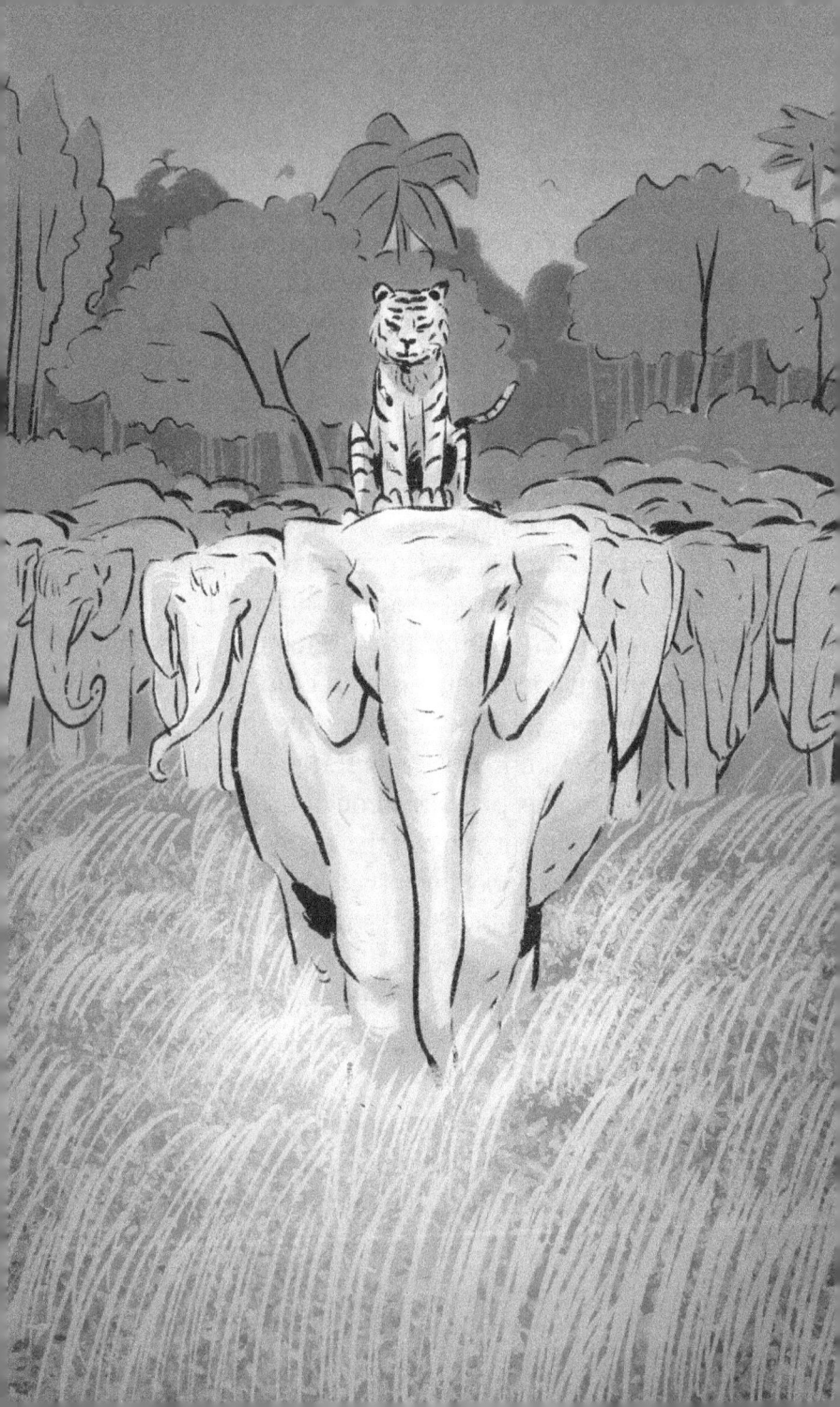

Hook Moustache also thought that he had, in his entire life, never experienced such an overpowering elephant smell. Sensing that danger was imminent, he asked the guards to be alert.

However bad the need to sleep was, if the officer asked them to be alert, the wardens couldn't but follow his orders. Picking up whatever came to hand, they all stood ready to do battle.

As per standard procedure, one of the guards took a big empty metal drum and started to beat it. Almost immediately, a noise was heard from the forest.

'Aha, there they are!'

Hook Moustache's finding was correct. An elephant came out of the forest and started nodding and swaying his head in tune with the drumming.

'What? You are trying to dance to the beat? Take out the crackers,' Hook Moustache screamed his order.

The wardens lit a large cracker and threw it into the forest. It hit the ground and burst after a few seconds but did not seem to make any difference.

After the cracker burst, one of the rail fences went flying through the air and smashed one of the floodlights. What followed was a hail of rail fence posts sending the wardens running for cover. Most of them chose to leap into the nearby river. Only Hook Moustache, who chose not to flee, saw the arrival of the elephants.

A huge elephant without tusks was leading the charge. Atop him was seated a tiger. Following them was an army of countless elephants emerging from the dense forest. Marshalling the army, an aged cow elephant stood to the side. Only now did Hook Moustache realise that the forest was home to so many elephants.

That was enough for him to run back into the guesthouse and bolt the doors. When he peeped through the window, what he saw was a dance of destruction.

All the fences were uprooted and flying through the air. The floodlight poles were pulled out, twisted around and smashed. The corral built using tall trees were brought down within minutes and Lightning Tusker was liberated.

A planned and well-coordinated attack by the elephants.

Unable to decide on the next steps, Hook Moustache lay down on the guesthouse floor with his eyes closed.

'Granny, shall we return now?' Tuskless Tusker asked her.

'No, there's one more thing left to do, my children. Right here is a genuine piece of the first share of Elephantam that we elephants received from the universe for ourselves. That's not for these men to keep.'

'What is that?' Lightning asked.

'Your father's tusks. They have kept it under lock and key somewhere in that building.'

Hook Moustache, lying on the floor scared out of wits, opened his eyes to the sounds of the tin roof cracking up. The elephants who had surrounded the guesthouse were pulling down the pillars and walls and bringing down the roof.

When the terrified Hook Moustache ran out of the building, something stopped him and then lifted him up. In the darkness when he felt it over, it was a huge elephant trunk. In that immovable state, he tried to see who the owner of the trunk was. It was him—that enormous mozha. One glimpse of the murderous look on his face, and Hook Moustache, without further ado, fainted.

Suddenly, however, in Tuskless Tusker, Misophantam surfaced. He wanted to do cruel things. The first one was to trample to death the forest ranger lying on the ground and squash his corpse.

Tuskless Tusker took two steps back and, with a bellow, lifted his foot. But before the foot could come down, two tusks appeared and blocked the foot. He looked angrily at the tusks that had dug into the ground and formed a frame over the fallen Hook Moustache, stopping him from completing the job. He saw that they belonged to his big brother. He saw lightning flash and rainbow colours gleam across them.

Testing each other's strength, both the tuskers maintained their stance. When she saw that, Granny was reminded of Elephantam and Misophantam warring with each other before the biggest explosion in elephant history.

'Elephantam must win, Misophantam must be defeated,' Granny mumbled.

Before she said it, Elephantam was already winning. Slowly, ever so slowly, the Elephantam that shone on Lightning's tusks defeated the Misophantam in Tuskless Tusker.

Once Misophantam had been suppressed, Tuskless Tusker came out of his murderous mood. When he saw that, Lightning caressed his little brother affectionately.

The elephants who had destroyed the forest office stood around, waiting. Lightning and his brother walked towards what was left of the building. Inside it was a special crate containing their father's tusks.

In one wallop, Tuskless Tusker smashed the crate with his trunk. Even in the darkness of the night, those tusks were resplendent with the colours of a peacock feather, as if they were live creatures.

Hook Moustache sat up in relief thinking, at least he was alive even if everything had been flattened. In his terror, his hook moustache drooped and became a walrus moustache. He could not believe his eyes as he sat there, looking at what lay in front of him. He rubbed his eyes and looked again.

With his tusks gleaming, Lightning walked in the front. Behind him was the tallest elephant in the world, with his head held high. From his long, curved tusks, a radiance enough to light up the entire forest beamed with the colours of peacock plume. A tiger was seated atop him, growling softly.

The other elephants were standing around in awe, watching the spectacle.

'Let's go back,' Granny Elephant gave the order.

The elephant army walked into the forest, following the two tuskers. Though the moon had set, the entire forest was bathed in divine light. The forest ranger felt that in that magical light, everything was fusing into one harmonious whole.

www.ingramcontent.com/pod-product-compliance
Lightning Source LLC
LaVergne TN
LVHW021224080526
838199LV00089B/5823